Ginny Morris and

Dad's New Girlfriend

Published by
MAGINATION PRESS
An Educational Publishing Foundation Book
American Psychological Association
750 First Street, NE
Washington, DC 20002

For more information about our books, including a complete catalog, please write to us,
call 1-800-374-2721, or visit our website at www.maginationpress.com.

Editor: Darcie Conner Johnston
Art Director: Susan K. White
The text type is New Baskerville
Printed by Worzalla, Stevens Point, Wisconsin

Library of Congress Cataloging-in-Publication Data

Gallagher, Mary Collins.
Ginny Morris and Dad's new girlfriend / by Mary Collins Gallagher ;
illustrated by Whitney Martin.
p. cm.
Summary: Just as Ginny begins to think that her divorced parents might like one another
again, she learns that her father has a girlfriend, and the mixture of feelings this stirs up
causes trouble at home and school—nearly ruining Halloween.
ISBN-13: 978-1-59147-386-2 (hardcover : alk. paper)
ISBN-10: 1-59147-386-1 (hardcover : alk. paper)
ISBN-13: 978-1-59147-387-9 (pbk : alk. paper)
ISBN-10: 1-59147-387-X (pbk. : alk. paper)
[1. Divorce—Fiction. 2. Schools—Fiction. 3. Friendship—Fiction.
4. Custody of children—Fiction.]
I. Martin, Whitney, 1968- ill. II. Title.
PZ7.G13617Ghv 2006
[Fic]—dc22   2005029256

10 9 8 7 6 5 4 3 2 1

Ginny Morris and
Dad's New Girlfriend

written by Mary Collins Gallagher

illustrated by Whitney Martin

MAGINATION PRESS • WASHINGTON, DC

For my big brother, Jerry — MCG

Chapter 1

If time traveling was a real thing, I'd zap back to the exact minute I asked my mom if I could take piano lessons, and I wouldn't ask that question. Because then Mom wouldn't have found Mrs. Winters right here in her apartment building, and I wouldn't be sitting in Mrs. Winters's living room right now, waiting to play "Waltz of the Sunflowers" in front of a bunch of dressed-up people.

My fingers wouldn't be tingling.

And I wouldn't be nervous about my parents,

who are divorced and not in the habit of being in the same room. Like they are right now. At this exact minute.

"Please, everyone find a seat," Mrs. Winters said, waving her arms around.

My face got hot.

I don't know how it happened. My mom and dad ended up only one cushion apart on the same couch. Tasha and Mitchell—they're my twin cousins—sat between them. But right away they slid to the floor to pet Mrs. Winters's cat, Dumpling.

I watched for trouble. I am very good at knowing when my parents are about to get mad at each other. Except I couldn't see their faces. They were turned, listening to Mrs. Winters.

"Classical music…talented pianists…children should practice…."

What I wanted more than anything was a drink of water to get the dry patch in the back of my throat wet again.

Too late. Drew Cameron was already playing "The Hunter's Song." He didn't mess up once.

I was next.

"My name is…uh, Ginny Morris."

Mom and Dad were nodding and smiling at me. For a second it seemed like they weren't even divorced. It felt like my heart was floating up to my throat. Somehow my fingers remembered what to do, and I played. Pretty well, I think.

After the recital, everyone was complimenting everyone. Mrs. Winters said "brilliant playing" to me, and I told her "great teaching."

"Did your mommy and daddy make up?" Tasha said, wrapping her little arms around my waist.

I almost choked on a bite of chocolate chip cookie. "What do you mean?" I whispered, and peeled her off.

"That's what Aunt Ellie said too."

"You asked my mom if she made up with my dad?"

"Uh-huh."

I groaned.

Then I noticed Dad, squatting like a frog, facing Mitchell.

I didn't like the looks of this.

"Me and Mitchell, we think Uncle Mark should move back with Aunt Ellie. We don't like it when you go to his house," she announced, like they had just been elected the little bosses of our family.

Ugh!

"Ready to go?" Dad said. Drops of sweat dotted his forehead.

"Okay, but I've got to get my stuff from Mom's."

I do joint custody with my parents, so it's a week with my mom, then a week with my dad, and on and on like that. Today is Sunday, switch day.

I gave Tasha a "don't say anything to Dad" look. But she's in first grade. I don't think she gets "looks" yet.

I waved to Mom. She was across the room talking to Aunt Lindsey and Uncle Bruce. They're the little bosses' parents. They live upstairs in 6B.

I hurried past Tasha and Mitchell, pulling Dad

with me. Mom caught up with us at the door.

"Don't forget to practice," Mrs. Winters said, and squeezed my hands. "I'll see you in a couple of weeks."

She's taking a break from teaching piano so she can go on a cruise with her sister. I just smiled. I don't plan on telling her that I'm taking a break from practicing.

Chapter 2

Instead of waiting in the lobby, Dad followed me and Mom into the elevator. Dad wiped his forehead. Mom took a big breath. They stood next to each other and didn't look mad at all.

"You were terrific," Mom said.

"The best," Dad said.

"Thanks." It was weird—them agreeing and sort of having a conversation.

Daisy met us at the door and barked like crazy at Dad.

"Daisy, Daisy, my old pal."

It only took a second for Daisy to start wagging her tail, jumping up on him, trying to lick him. That dog's got a good memory.

I went to my room and checked over my **Do Not Forget** list. Before I zipped my bag I put Leroy, my stuffed monkey, on top. Leroy lives with me wherever I am.

Then I stood in the hall and listened for other things they might be saying to each other. Maybe what the twins did wasn't so bad. Maybe Mom and Dad are becoming friends again. Maybe....

"I've missed you...." I think that's what I heard Dad say!

I had to look.

He was petting Daisy. But Mom was standing there too. And their faces looked calm. I got that "maybe" feeling again.

Mom was her smiley self, but I knew she was kind of sad about me leaving. I was too. We won't be with each other for a whole week, and on top of that, Halloween is Friday. She really likes seeing me in my costume. I told her we'd take pictures. I hate the feeling I get when I leave my mom.

Chapter 3

"You miss Daisy a lot, don't you, Dad?"

"Yeah, I guess I do."

"Why don't you come over and see her more often, like on piano lesson days? You could wait for me in Mom's apartment." They'd sit on the couch, talk about the good old times…. Who knows what might happen?

"That's something to think about," he said as we drove up to the house.

I thought the day would finally settle down once

I got to Dad's. But actually, it just got weirder. The first thing was the leaves were gone. Last week, the yard looked like it was covered with corn flakes. Dad said I had to rake, but I knew we'd do it together.

"Dad, the leaves?"

"I didn't think you'd mind getting out of a little work."

"Well, no, but...." Then I saw two carved pumpkins by the front door.

"Dad! You carved pumpkins without me?"

"I thought you'd like the surprise. Anyway, there are two more for you to do."

"But...."

How could he not know that pumpkin carving is one of my favorite things?

"Gosh, honey. It seemed like a good idea."

"Hmmph" was all I managed to get out.

And the bushes looked like they got a haircut.

When I stepped into the living room, I thought I had it figured out. "Grandma's coming, isn't she?" I couldn't think of any other reason why the house would be this spotless.

Charlie meowed and weaved through my legs.

"No, Ginny, I just cleaned up. A friend came over for dinner."

"Really?" It didn't surprise me that Dad had a friend over, just that he'd go nuts cleaning the house for one.

I picked up Charlie and looked into his yellow eyes for a clue about why Dad was acting so different.

And then it turned out that still wasn't everything. My room was sort of cleaned up too! You could see the floor. My books were stacked up on the desk, and my rocks, which I used to collect, were spread out on my dresser.

It didn't feel like my room. It didn't seem like my house.

Dad stood in the doorway with his arms folded over his chest.

I folded my arms too, and gave him a "what the heck is going on?" look.

"It was a mess in here, Ginny. How about keeping your room a little neater from now on?"

"Dad, this is my room—my private room."

"Yes, it is. But your private room looked like the debris field from a tornado."

"You could have just shut the door. Who'd you have over? The President?"

He laughed. "It was someone I work with—a woman."

"What kind of woman?"

He laughed again. "A grown-up, human-girl kind of woman."

I sucked my cheeks in so I wouldn't laugh.

"She's a friend who is a woman," he said.

"A friend friend?"

"Her name is Ruth. She's very nice."

I thought about Dominic, my friend who is a boy, and how annoyed I get when kids say he's my boyfriend. So I decided to go along with Dad about it. Except I was still mad about the pumpkins.

"Okay. But she wasn't in my room, was she?"

"Not really. She just peeked in." Now he was grinning.

"Da-ad!"

Then he changed the subject by asking me to go for a bike ride, which is what we usually do on switch days. But nothing felt usual around here. It was kind of like my house and my dad got traded for another house and dad that looked the same but really weren't. All I wanted to do was curl up with Charlie.

"No, thanks. I'm kind of tired," I told him.

I must have really been tired because I conked right out.

Chapter 4

When I woke up, it was dark. It took me a
second, but then I sniffed one of my most favorite
dinners. Lasagna! My dad is a very good cook—a
very good organic cook, that is. He's the deli chef
at Obido's Organic Foods. Preservatives and
artificial ingredients are like poison ivy to him.

Dad was on the phone when I walked into the
kitchen. He waved and mouthed the words, "I'll be
off in a few minutes." While he was talking, he set a
plate of lasagna on the table in front of me. His

cheeks were pink and he was smiling. It didn't seem like the smile was for me.

"Who is it?" I mouthed back to him.

"Ruth."

"I'll wait for you," I said out loud.

But he didn't answer. He was listening to her.

Then he started laughing. "That is so funny," he said into the phone.

I scraped my fork across the plate. He didn't even look at me.

I made a loud clearing-my-throat sound, but he kept right on talking. And he didn't get off the phone in a few minutes, even though I haven't been here for a whole week!

I didn't feel hungry anymore for his stupid lasagna. The only thing I felt was invisible.

●　　●　　●

I went back to my room and looked over my homework. Every Monday my teacher, Mr. Gorski, gives us a big packet of assignments, which we have a whole week to do. If you're "organized and focused" (two of Mr. Gorski's favorite words), you get it done by Friday and have the weekend for fun.

Mom's real hyper when it comes to homework— she is an English teacher at the community college—so when I'm at her house I usually just go ahead and do it while she grades papers. But I hadn't finished this week because of practicing piano so much.

Mr. Gorski always gives us ten of every kind of

problem to do. He says it's because most of us are ten years old. I don't think that's a good reason for making us do so much work. I think five would be enough, and that would go with the grade we're in—fifth.

So I put that idea in the suggestion box on the third day of school. When he read it out loud, everybody clapped. He said he'd think about it, but we knew we'd be stuck doing ten all year. When adults say they'll think about it, you might as well forget it.

Math: ten fraction addition problems.

Easy. Did that already.

Vocabulary: find ten words that contain the excellent letter X.

I still had two words to go. I flipped through my dictionary and wrote the definitions.

Perplexed: puzzled or unsure
Vexed: annoyed or irritated

I shoved the paper into my language arts folder. I also have a science report on space and time travel due in a couple weeks, but I wasn't in the mood for working on it. Usually that's a subject I'm very interested in. But not tonight.

I dumped my bag out on the floor to find my journal. It was starting to look like my room again.

So many feelings were swimming around in my head that I wanted to write to Grammy about them. She was my great-grandma Virginia. She died when I was in third grade, but I write to her anyway. Thinking about how she liked listening to me makes it easy to write down things I have on my mind.

Dear Grammy,

Today when Mom and Dad sat by each other and talked to each other, I thought that maybe they will start liking each other again and maybe, just maybe, they'll even get back together. But now I am sooooo perplexed. It feels like aliens took my dad and replaced him with a clone who's a cleaning freak and who acts different and who cares more about talking on the phone to his friend who is a woman than he does about me. I'm mad at him. I'm vexed.

I wish Mrs. Winters would let me play some un-classical music for a change. I might want to be a keyboard player in a rock band sometime.

Ginny

Chapter 5

Charlie circled my head, purring.

Ugh. Monday morning.

"Go away," I told him, but he started licking my cheek with his scratchy little tongue, so I got up.

I heard whistling and staggered into the kitchen.

"Good morning, Sunshine," Dad said, all cheery.

This was not normal. My dad is not a morning person. I looked hard at him, remembering that I was mad. But it's not easy to stay mad at a person who's in a really good mood, especially when he's making blueberry pancakes.

I heard knocking. Rebecca was peeking through the window in the kitchen door. I forgot she was coming over early to talk about our Halloween costumes. We're not in the same classroom, so we don't have much time together at school.

"Hi, Mr. Morris."

"Good morning to you!" He was practically singing.

Rebecca gave me a "what's up with your dad?" look. I made a circle around my ear. If it was any-body but Rebecca seeing my dad acting so weird, I'd be really embarrassed.

Then she looked at me—my whole me. "Get dressed!" she kind of yelled, which didn't bother me because I knew she wasn't mad. We're best friends. I kind of yell at her sometimes too.

"Okay, okay." I shoveled in one more forkful.

Dad handed her a plate of pancakes.

"Take your time," she said, pouring syrup.

•　•　•

We had to run for the bus, without having a second to talk about our costumes.

"Let's go to my house after school," Rebecca panted as the bus door swung back open for us. "We'll see what we can find in the attic. Maybe we'll get some ideas."

"All right! It's a Ginny week!" That's what Mr. Bilby said. He's our bus driver. I don't take the bus when I'm at Mom's, and he's always glad to see me on the weeks when I'm at Dad's. I like that.

"Hi, Mr. Bilby." We gave each other five.

Dominic waved. He was in the back with the other fifth-grade boys. We sat next to each other all last year. We had to because of a seating chart Mr. Bilby made. Sometimes I wish we still had that chart. Then Dominic and I could sit together without getting teased. I'm tired of telling people we're just friends.

When we got off the bus, I walked real slow so Dominic could catch up with me. He's in my classroom, which is almost as good as having Rebecca.

"How was it at your dad's?" I asked him. His parents are divorced too.

"Kind of fun. How was your piano thing?"

"Good. My parents were even nice to each other."

"Whoa."

"But—my dad." We stopped outside the classroom door. "He had some woman over for dinner when I was at my mom's. I think he likes her."

"Likes her?"

"He said they were friends."

"That's what my mom said about Steve. But pretty soon they were holding hands. And kissing."

"Eeeuw. Right in front of you?"

He laughed and nodded. I laughed too, but I got a weird feeling in my stomach.

The tardy buzzer went off. Mr. Gorski was standing in the doorway. "Hey, you two, planning to come to school today?"

Chapter 6

Charlie was waiting by the door for me. He has this way of knowing when I'm about to get home. Dad said it's because Charlie is a creature of habit. But I think he could be a psychic cat. I scooped him up, and we meowed at each other.

Mrs. Howard was on the couch. She's a lady who Dad says is watching over the house—not me. Actually, what she really watches is TV. She had her favorite soap opera on, and she was all engrossed in it.

"Hi, Mrs. Howard." I sat next to her.

"Hello, dear."

I glanced at the TV. "Did Louise find out about Donald yet?"

"Not yet...." She looked at me. "Homework?"

"Yeah, I've got a bunch of it."

●　　●　　●

I pulled out this week's assignments.

Math: measure the circumference of ten round objects in your house

Vocabulary: find ten more words containing the excellent letter X.

Sheesh. Mr. Gorski doesn't have much imagination when it comes to vocabulary words. I picked up the dictionary and found two excellent words.

Flummoxed: very confused

Oxymoron: words put together that seem to contradict each other; a wise fool or loud silence

Sitting in my room with the dictionary was too boring, so I decided to move on to the Ten Round Objects assignment before going to Rebecca's. I measured an orange, a cantaloupe, and got hungry so I ate half of each. One of the stupid carved pumpkins was almost round, so I measured it too.

My last stop was the garage. Mrs. Howard and I, we figured that garages are parts of people's houses, especially if they're attached, like ours is. I found enough different sized balls in there to get it done.

Halloween is only four days away, which means Rebecca and I have that many days to keep our costumes a secret. But first we have to figure out what we're going to be.

Last year most of the kids around here, us included, were magical wizards. Too bad I'll never get to wear that costume again. It was a great costume, my best so far. One of my secret wishes is for our school, Thoreau Elementary, to become a school that teaches magic. Or time travel.

We wanted to get in and out of her attic before dark. Rebecca's mom said it's just the wind and maybe a few squirrels making all that noise at night. I don't know why parents always go for the boring explanations, when no one knows for sure.

We checked the rafters—no bats that we could see—and got busy searching through the trunks. There are a bunch of them, and they're filled with old clothes and stuff from when her parents and her grandparents were younger.

"I'm wearing this for sure," she said, putting on an army jacket.

"Cool."

I found a feathery little hat and a button with a peace sign on it.

She pulled a long skirt over her jeans.

I was trying on a pair of cowboy boots when we

heard The Whistle. It was my dad. If he gets home and doesn't know where I am, that's what he does. Carlton—he's Rebecca's twelve-year-old brother—said my dad could maybe even get into the *Guinness Book of World Records* for how loud he can whistle.

Chapter 7

Lasagna tastes better the second day. At least my dad's does. I was on my second plateful.

"Oh, remember Ruth, the friend I told you about?" he said.

I nodded. How could I not remember?

"She's bringing dessert over."

The mound of noodles and cheese I was about to swallow stopped in the back of my throat, and my eyes got watery like they do right before I throw up.

"You okay?" he said.

I gulped hard and got it down. "You mean she's coming over now?"

"She'll be here any minute." He looked like he'd just won the lottery or something.

About a second later the doorbell rang.

Before I had a chance to bolt out the door, there she was, standing next to Dad. She had that all-natural look, like Dad. It was weird how they kind of matched. I bet she loves tofu.

She held her hand out and I shook it. Sort of.

"Call me Ruth," she said, all friendly. Then she offered me a cookie, probably organic.

"Not right now. Thanks anyway. Uh…Dad, can I go to Rebecca's?"

Dad's smile disappeared, and I felt guilty for what I was thinking, which was that I wish Ruth did not exist in any dimension of space-time.

"Sure, but don't stay long," he said, kind of squinting, like he was trying to figure me out.

"Talk to you later," Ruth said.

I waved and backed out the door.

So Rebecca is my best friend, and I totally expected her to be shocked, like I was. Only she wasn't.

"Well, is she nice?"

"No. I mean, I don't know."

"What does she look like?"

I shrugged.

"Well, you said you met her."

"Yeah, but…."

"Well, come on. Let's go." She was grinning, like

this was something funny we had to check out.

"No."

But all I could do was follow her across the yard and through the door to our kitchen.

They were sitting so close to each other at the table that their chairs were touching. I think their hands were touching too. When we came through the door they stood up really fast.

Right away, Rebecca (who is into jewelry) complimented Ruth on her dolphin earrings, which were dangling almost to her shoulders. I thought they looked dumb, even though I do like dolphins.

Ruth kept turning her head to smile at Rebecca and then at me, which made the dolphins look like they were flying. It didn't seem like Ruth was fake smiling, but it would have been fake if I smiled back at her. Rebecca and Dad were smiling too. All this smiling was making me sick!

When Dad started to rinse off the plates, Ruth started filling the dishwasher, like I usually do. Suddenly, I wanted to talk to my mom.

I went to the study and pushed the numbers. It rang and rang until I heard my own voice. "Hi. Ginny, Ellie, and Daisy aren't home right now. Please leave a message." I bit my lip and made myself go back into the kitchen.

"I've got a lot of homework," I told them.

Rebecca said she did too, and gave me a "what's wrong?" look.

I shrugged. I didn't know exactly what was wrong. But I knew something was.

"See ya tomorrow."

Chapter 8

Dear Grammy,

I'm afraid Dad really does have a girlfriend. I don't think I should tell Mom about it. It might hurt her feelings, or maybe she'd be mad. And would it be like gossiping about Dad if I did tell her? How will Mom and Dad ever get back together with Ruth bringing over organic cookies and smiling at him like that? Disgusting!! I wish I could go back through space-time to when Dad met Ruth. I'd stop it from happening.

I wonder if Mom and Dad ever looked at each other like that. I have a real bad feeling about this.

Ginny

I'd gotten through five more excellent letter X words when Dad leaned into my room.

"Working hard?"

"Mm-hmm."

"Sorry we didn't get around to carving those pumpkins."

"Yeah."

"Ruth is nice, don't you think?"

"I guess."

He was so into how nice Ruth is that he didn't even notice how not myself I was acting.

"I think you'll really like her once you get to know her."

I wanted to tell him that I don't want to get to know her.

"I've got to get this done, Dad."

"Okay. We'll do that carving tomorrow, for sure."

"Whatever." Who cares about stupid pumpkins anyway?

I turned on my computer. There was an email from Mom.

Monday night

Hi Ginny,

Hope you had a good day. Are you and your dad getting ready for Halloween?

I know it's a fun week, but don't forget to work on that homework packet.

Daisy and I miss you!!

Love you,
Mom

Hi Mom,

I really miss you. I've been thinking…maybe I should live with just you, and come over here once in awhile. That's how Dominic does it, and he said it's not so confusing that way. I really wish I could see you.

Love,
Ginny

I pushed SEND, and felt a little better—for one second. Then I felt terrible for saying I didn't want to live with Dad.

Mom- that email I just sent? Forget about it. I'm just having a weird week. But I do miss you. Ginny

---

A couple minutes later the phone rang.
"Ginny, your mom's on the phone."
Uh-oh. "I'll get it in the study, Dad."

Me: Hi, Mom.

Mom: Ginny, what's wrong?

Me: Nothing. Really.

Mom: Are you and your dad having a problem?

Me: No, I'm just feeling a little weird, that's all.

Mom: What are you feeling weird about?

Me: Umm...sometimes I get different feelings, for no reason.

Mom: Oh. (She was quiet for a couple seconds.) Remember the film you saw last year, about growing up?

Me: Yeah.

Mom: It could be hormones.

Me: (I laughed.) Mo-om.

Mom: (Mom laughed too.) Well, whatever it is, maybe you need some time to think about it? I hope you'll always feel like talking to me when something's on your mind.

Me: I will, Mom.

Chapter 9

"I like your dad's girlfriend." That was the first thing Rebecca said to me at the bus stop.

"Who said she's his girlfriend?"

"Well, it looked like it."

I felt my face pinch up.

"If my parents were divorced," she went on, "I'd want my dad to have a girlfriend. It'd almost be like having a mom at both places. And she even kind of looks like you. You've got the same hair."

My heart started pounding and my hands got

tense. I felt like shoving her. "Well, your parents aren't divorced! You don't know anything about it!"

Rebecca's mouth fell open. Mine did too. I think we were both surprised by how mean I sounded.

She closed her mouth and glared at me and then walked off, all huffy.

When the bus pulled up, Rebecca ran to the back and sat with Marina Lewis.

I stomped by Mr. Bilby without saying hi, and plopped into a seat next to a second grader who smelled like peanut butter.

After morning announcements we had gym. The first thing was running ten laps. Our reward was getting to play basketball, which is one of my favorite sports. But I had on a sweatshirt, with no t-shirt under it. I was boiling. I was ready to pass out. I didn't make one basket.

When we got back to the classroom, Mr. Gorski announced that we were going to work in groups of three to find round stuff in the classroom to measure. He said he was going to divide us up alphabetically, which meant that I'd be stuck with best-friend-stealing Marina Lewis and with Devon Loman, who makes animal sounds all the time.

While everyone was dragging desks around to form their groups, I walked up to Mr. Gorski. I felt really, really sick. So sick, I told him, that I was about to throw up. And I meant it. He looked me over, trying to decide if I was faking, and handed me a pass to go to the nurse.

Chapter 10

"No fever, but you do look a bit ragged,"
Mrs. Bruno said. "Who are you with this week?"
She knows everything about everybody's family.

I knew I'd get in big trouble for what I was about
to say, but I went ahead and said it anyway. "My
mom's. Uh, could I call her?"

"Sure, sweetie."

I stared at the numbers on the phone.

"Did you forget your mother's work number?"

"No." I sighed and pushed 7-1-9-5-7-5. I took a

deep breath and tapped the last number—1— really fast, like it was on fire.

"Hello, this is Ellie Morris," she said in her teacher voice.

"Hi, Mom."

"Ginny?"

"Yeah, ummm. I'm sick—it's my stomach—and uh dad's uh busy uh…at work." It wasn't a total lie. Dad probably was really busy.

"Oh, honey. It may take awhile. But I'll be there," she said.

Mrs. Bruno told me to rest on the cot in her room. I tried to count the tiles on the ceiling, but I kept thinking about Dad looking all lovey-dovey at Ruth, about how mad Rebecca and I were at each other, and about how mad Mom would be at me. It felt like my stomach was tied into a big knot that was getting tighter by the minute.

I was seriously wishing that I could take back calling Mom. Maybe I'd call her cell phone. But it was too late. There she was, standing in the door-way.

"Oh, honey." She hugged me and felt my head.

When we got home, Mom tucked me in and brought me ginger ale and read me a chapter of one of my favorite books, *A Single Shard*. It's a story about an orphan in Korea, and he's living in the twelfth century, which was almost a thousand years ago. I love trying to imagine what things were like so long ago. And on the other side of the world too.

It felt really good to be there with Mom. I didn't

even care that I'd probably be grounded for the next ten years.

"Get some rest," she said, fluffing up my pillow. "I think I'll give your dad a call and let him know how you're doing."

"Uh, uh, Mom?" I said in a croaky voice, but she'd already walked out of the room. Now I was wishing that I could travel through space-time to Korea or to the twelfth century—anywhere but here and now.

I patted my bed. "Daisy, come here. Save me." She jumped on my bed, and I let her lick my face.

Mom was on the phone in the living room, which in our little apartment is practically outside my bedroom door.

"What?" she said, sounding totally flummoxed. "She didn't?"

I pulled the blanket over my head and plugged my ears.

Chapter 11

"We need to talk, young lady." Being called young lady was a bad sign. I peeked over the top of the blanket. Mom was staring at me.

I stared at the blanket

"Ginny, what's going on?"

"Uh," I shrugged.

"I had to cancel a class to pick you up. Your dad said you didn't even call him." She looked confused. She might have even looked a little mad.

"I wanted to come over here."

"I don't understand. Are you sick?" She sat on my bed.

"Yeah, but it's the kind of sick I used to get all the time when you and Dad first got divorced."

"Is there something going on now that's making you feel that way?"

So I told her about Dad and Ruth and about my fight with Rebecca.

Her face got softer.

"Ginny, it's natural for your dad to meet someone."

"It doesn't feel natural to me. Dad's acting weird. For one thing, he turned into a cleaning freak."

Mom laughed. "Now that's hard to imagine."

"He did—really. It doesn't even feel like my house anymore."

"You need to talk to him about this."

"I don't want to talk to him. I wish I could just stay with you, Mom."

"Honey, you know I love having you here. But this is your dad's week. You'll feel better once you tell him how you're feeling."

"I feel better now that I talked to *you*. I don't think I want to talk to him."

"I'm sure it does feel really different over there right now. And I can understand that you feel uncomfortable. But Ginny, he's your dad, no matter what."

"I know."

"I'm sure he'll listen when you talk to him tonight."

"Do I have to?"

She just looked at me. "And honey, unless you're really sick, I need to go back to work, and you need to be in school."

I was afraid she was going to say that.

I groaned.

"But let's have lunch together first."

"Can we get tacos at the drive-thru?"

"Sure," she said, grinning. "You must be feeling better if you're up for a taco."

Chapter 12

Fifth graders were streaming out the cafeteria door when I got there. At least I didn't miss recess.

By the time I got to the soccer field, they were already divided into teams—Devon, Katy, Lena, and those guys, playing against my friends. Dominic and Shannon were forwards, Rebecca and Patrick were on goal, and the sides were even. That meant I couldn't play unless someone dropped out. So I watched.

Devon dribbled down the field and took a

lopsided shot on the goal. Rebecca batted it away like a first grader had kicked it. "Way to go, Rebecca," I yelled. I hoped she heard me.

Katy jogged toward me. "I've gotta go. Want to play for me?"

Playing on Devon's team was better than not playing at all. At least I thought it was until I got out there, and he gave me one of his "I'm the boss" looks. "You're wing. Don't give the ball away to your boyfriend."

He took off before I could say anything.

I sprinted down the sideline. We yelled at Devon to pass, but he kept hogging the ball. Dominic closed in and popped it out from under him. It rolled my way. Dominic and I were dueling for it and laughing. But our legs got tangled, and we fell. Suddenly we were serious. All I wanted to do was get that ball. Me and Dominic and Shannon—we were going for it but I got there first and sent it downfield.

Lena kicked it, but the ball bounced off the goal post.

Rebecca bolted out of the goal.

I ran full speed and kicked it with everything I had. It flew like a canon ball—right into her face. The game stopped. She was crying, and blood was pouring out of her nose.

"Rebecca, are you okay?" I felt like crying too.

She didn't hear me because her team (which should have been my team) crowded around her.

Devon tried to give me a high-five, but I kept my hands down.

Then Ms. Riley—she was my teacher last year—came over and hurried Rebecca into the building. Nobody said it was my fault. But nobody said it wasn't either. Even Dominic was giving me a mean look, so I gave one back to him.

"What's wrong with you?" he said.

"What's wrong with you?" I said.

Mr. Gorski gave me a "so you *were* faking" look.

"Uh, Mr. Gorski, could I go to the nurse's office?"

"Again?" He looked tired.

I wanted to go see if Rebecca was all right, but he told me not to worry, Mrs. Bruno would take care of her.

So I had to sit there and listen to him read *My Side of the Mountain* to the class. Maybe that's what I'll do—find my own mountain to live on!

During writing workshop, Mr. Gorski heard Shannon call Patrick an oxymoron, so he stopped everything to give us his "respecting ourselves and others" talk. Then we got a vocabulary lesson. We had to think of examples of oxymorons. "Here's one," he said, "healthy Halloween treats."

Well, that only got me in a worse mood, because it reminded me that my dad really would be giving out healthy Halloween treats.

A folded-up piece of paper hit me on the arm and landed on my desk.
I opened it.

What's your dad giving out? health nut bars?

I turned around. Dominic was grinning. He knows all about my dad's natural food thing.

I grinned back.

Rebecca wasn't on the bus. That got me really worried. No one was next to Dominic, so I sat with him. Marina made that stupid "ooooh" sound, but I didn't care. I ate Dominic's leftover Cheetos and told him about Ruth and about being in trouble. Dominic said he got used to his mom having a boyfriend, and they hardly ever kiss in front of him anymore. And he told me that he got a little mad when I beat him at soccer. But he was over it.

When I got off the bus I went right up to Rebecca's door. I wanted to tell her that I was sorry. Maybe she'd say sorry too, and we could go back to being friends. I hate being in fights with Rebecca.

I knocked. Carlton opened the door and looked down at me. He's taller than my dad, even though he's only twelve.

"Is Rebecca here?"

"Nope. She's with my mom somewhere."

"Tell her I came over to see if she's okay. Okay?"

"Okay." Suddenly Carlton looked at me like he'd just remembered that I was an ax murderer or something. "I heard you tried to kill her."

This day was not getting any better.

Chapter 13

I said a really quick hi to Mrs. Howard and went to my room. I looked through my homework packet. There was only social studies, and one more vocabulary word to find.

I flipped through the E's in the dictionary, looking for another X word. There are about a billion E words with the letter X in them.

Exonerate: to declare that somebody is not to blame, or is not guilty of a crime

Exonerated! That's what I wanted to be.

Then I heard Dad's voice. He was home early.

I put down my pencil. I could feel him standing behind me.

"Ginny, can we talk?"

I turned around and nodded.

He sat on my bed.

"Dad, I'm sorry I didn't call you."

"Your mom told me why you didn't."

I didn't know what to say.

"I didn't realize that my dating Ruth would be this hard on you."

I took a big breath and let it out. "Dad—one minute it's you and me, and the next minute Ruth is there and everything feels all different. And you seem different too."

"Honey, Ruth and I have been going out for awhile. I thought it was time for you to meet her."

"For awhile? How long is that? You should have told me."

"I wanted to wait until I was pretty sure that she and I would keep seeing each other. There was no reason to tell you any sooner."

"Well, it's too soon for me. Or too fast. Or too something. And what about how nice you and Mom are being to each other?" I surprised myself when I said that.

"Your mom and I are friends." He patted my arm, like he wanted me to know that he understood how I felt. "And we both love you."

"Yeah, I know." I got an empty feeling. Suddenly I knew for sure that they would never get back together. Not ever.

"I like Ruth and enjoy spending time with her. I hope you'll give her a chance."

I wanted to crawl away and curl up with Charlie, but I managed to say I would try. "Does she have to come over all the time, though?"

"No, Ginny, she doesn't have to come over all the time."

After dinner Dad covered the kitchen table with newspapers, and we carved the pumpkins. We tried to act like we were in a good mood.

Dear Grammy,

I reeeaallly wish I was a time traveler so I could zap back to when I woke up this morning and do the whole day over!!!!

I'm glad Dominic and I aren't in a fight. But if we became enemies and never liked each other again, I think I would still hate it if he got a new best friend who's a girl. I wonder how Mom really feels about Dad and Ruth. I wonder if she kind of wants to get back with Dad. I wonder if she'll be jealous if I get used to Ruth and even start liking her. I wonder if Rebecca and I will get to be friends again. All this wondering is driving me CRAZY!

I haven't talked to the counselor since our divorce group in third grade. Maybe I'll ask her if she has a group for kids who have to give up hoping their parents will get back together. Because I think that's what I have to do.

Ginny

Chapter 14

Hi Ginny,

I've been thinking about how you might be feeling--about your dad and me. I know kids usually want their parents to get back together. Your dad and I get along, but honey--believe me--he and I are not made to live together. It'll take time to get used to your dad having someone new in his life. It may even take me awhile. But please be polite--and go ahead and like her--if she's nice. And I'll bet she is.

Did you and Rebecca make up?

Love you,
Mom

p.s. Happy Halloween! Have fun tomorrow. Save some candy for me!

Thanks, Mom.
I love you a lot!
Ginny

p.s. On Tuesday, I accidentally kicked Rebecca in the face with the soccer ball, and now we are totally ignoring each other. I don't know if we'll even be going trick-or-treating together.

Chapter 15

"Da-ad! We overslept!"

He opened an eye and looked up at me.

"It's me, Ginny, your daughter."

He cracked a smile. "Glad to know you, Ginny."

"I'm going to miss the bus!"

"I'll drive you," he said, rubbing his eyes.

It's amazing how much better you can feel after a good night's sleep, Grammy used to say, and I had to admit she was right. I was in a pretty good mood. Even though I still hadn't made up with

Rebecca, and even though Dad probably still liked Ruth.

In the car I started thinking. Probably I'll never want Dad to go out with anyone except Mom. But I had to admit there's no way to stop him. And Mom seems to be okay with it. And he's a lot more fun when he's happy. So maybe I could try to get used to it, like Dominic did with his mom's boyfriend.

"Okay, Dad," I said.

"Okay what, honey?"

"Okay about Ruth."

We stopped in front of the school.

He looked at me with his head tilted, trying to figure me out.

"You mean about me seeing her, or about you seeing her?"

"Both, I guess."

He smiled. "I really appreciate your giving it a try."

"But will you let me know, way ahead of time, at least a whole day, if she's coming over?"

"You've got it."

"And can we still have time together, just you and me?"

"Absolutely. We will always have time together, Ginny. That's important to me too. But let's agree that you'll let me know whenever you need extra, okay?"

"I will. And…." I had to say this part but I didn't want to. "No mushy stuff in front of me, please?"

He tilted his head and said, "What do you mean?"

"Da-ad!"

He laughed. "I understand."

•   •   •

It started raining during math and poured all through lunch. The lunch ladies gave us pumpkin-shaped cookies and turned on the movie *Snow White*, which they've shown us at least fifty times. They said Halloween movies might scare the little kids. Oh brother. As if that evil queen stepmother isn't scary! But I am not even going to think about stepmothers.

Rebecca's class was three tables away. I could only see the back of her head until our teachers came to pick us up. When she turned around I saw how purplish-green the skin around her eye had gotten. It was gross. She didn't look at me.

I was feeling sick again, but going to the nurse didn't seem like a good idea.

When we were done with social studies, the room parents came with more cookies and made us play BATS Bingo. I was the first to get BATS. I won a plastic skull ring. Then it stopped raining, and Mr. Gorski let us go outside. Normally, those kinds of things cheer me up, but I kept seeing Rebecca's bruised-up face in my mind.

After school she was already on the bus—in the back, with Marina—when I got there. I sat up front by Mr. Bilby. He smiled really nice at me. I knew he knew I was having a crummy week.

When I got off the bus, I waited for Rebecca.

But it pulled away, with her on it. She was probably going home with Marina and probably going trick-or-treating with her too. Guess I'll be passing out raisins and trail mix to kids who will look at me like I'm giving them dog food.

Dad wasn't home from work, and I didn't feel like talking to Mrs. Howard or writing to Grammy.

Dear Rebecca,

I am very very very sorry the soccer ball hit you. I saw your eye and it must hurt like crazy. And I saw how your nose was bleeding too. I feel terrible about it, even though I was trying to make a goal, not hurt you.

AND I am sorry I got so mad about you saying my dad has a girlfriend and that other stuff. You're right. He does have a girlfriend. Can we please be friends again? I miss you!

Ginny

Chapter 16

I was looking for an envelope when the doorbell rang. "Ginny, dear…," Mrs. Howard called.

It was Rebecca. She was telling Mrs. Howard what happened to her eye.

"I thought you were at Marina's?"

"I was, but I decided to come home."

"This is for you." I handed her the letter.

She read it.

"You were just playing a good game. I should have put my hands up."

I let out a breath. "Does it hurt?"

"Only when I touch it. Uh…my mom said I shouldn't have said what I said about your dad having a girlfriend, and about her being like a mom. Sorry."

"That's okay. Sorry I got so mad."

"That's okay. Are you going trick-or-treating?" she said.

I shrugged. "Are you?"

She shrugged too.

"Want to?"

We did, and right away we got the idea of going back to her attic for costumes.

Mrs. Romano—she's Rebecca's mom—gave me an "I'm so glad you two are friends again" look. She said we could use any of the clothes in the trunks as long as we were careful with them. We'd be wearing the family's history.

It wasn't dark outside, but there was no light in that attic.

We inched toward the center of the room to find the chain to turn on the light.

A scratching sound came from somewhere.

"What's that?" I whispered.

"I don't know."

Then we heard another sound, like breathing. Heavy breathing.

We grabbed each other's arms.

Something black was moving toward us.

"Let's get out of here," I squeaked.

At that instant, a beam of light flashed on right in front of us, shining on a white face.

"I vant your blood," the face said.

"Carlton, get a life!"

Rebecca turned on the light.

"You guys were so scared."

"Were not," Rebecca said.

"Cool vampire costume," I told him.

Carlton let us use his monster make-up kit, and we made our faces green, to go with the color around Rebecca's eye.

Chapter 17

"Come over after dinner," I told Rebecca, and ran out the door.

I was still on her porch when I saw Dad. He was standing by a car. And Ruth was in it.

I waited till she drove off. Then I marched up to Dad and gave him a "you broke your promise" look.

"I didn't know she was coming over. But I'll bet you'll be glad she did."

"Huh? Why would I be glad?"

I followed him into the house.

Dad pointed to a bowl on the coffee table. It was filled with candy, real candy: Tootsie Pops, Snickers, Twizzlers.

"Ruth brought it." He looked at it like it was a bowl of snakes.

"I thought she was all-natural and organic, like you."

"You know what she said?" he started smiling. "She said it *is* all-natural to have candy on Halloween."

I laughed. "Dad, she's right." And funny too, I thought. I was glad she came over. "We are going to pass this candy out, aren't we?"

"Maybe. We'll give the kids a choice."

I laughed again. "Okay, Dad. But now I have to get dressed!"

• • •

Dad was holding a camera when I came into the kitchen to grab a pre-trick-or-treat apple. One last healthy thing before the candy begins.

"Let's take a picture of you in your…what kind of costume is that, anyway?" said Dad.

"See if you can guess. Just pretend this isn't Halloween and this isn't a costume. I came home wearing this funny old hat, this skirt with a poodle on it, this army shirt and this vest, and the button with a peace sign. Why am I wearing this stuff? Where do you think I got it?"

"From Rebecca's attic?"

58

"Dad, use your imagination. Okay, here's another clue. Some people who know a lot about black holes and space-time and dimensions and stuff like that think it might be possible. Remember the astronomy books I've been reading for my science project?"

"I'm really confused."

"Time traveling, Dad! Rebecca and I, we're pretending we went back in time and got these clothes. We're time travelers."

"Great idea! But what's with the green face?"

"We're zombie time travelers."

"Right," he said. "We need a record of this for the future."

I looked at the bowl of candy and smiled.

When Your Parents Start to Date
by MARY LAMIA, Ph.D.

As you read *Ginny Morris and Dad's New Girlfriend*, some of
Ginny's experiences may seem familiar. Is one of your
parents dating? If so, Ginny's story may help you feel less
alone with what you're going through. When divorced parents
start to see new friends, parents may seem like total strangers,
behaving in ways their kids have never seen. It's not unusual
for kids to feel left out, uncomfortable, and confused.

CHANGES IN YOUR PARENT

Sometimes parents act differently when they meet someone
they like. They may seem happier or distracted. You probably
know how that is, because it's just like when you get excited
about having a new friend or a crush.

But it seems strange when a parent is behaving differently.
They might talk on the phone too long or smile a lot or seem
like their minds are elsewhere. You want your parents to be
happy, but it's confusing when they are happier because they
like someone who is not your other parent.

When parents start dating a new friend, they can be self-
absorbed for a little while. They are thinking about themselves
as they adjust to a different life, just as you are. They are not
intentionally ignoring you. However, if you feel left out or
annoyed or upset (or "vexed," like Ginny), it's important to
find a way to let them know that you still need their love,
attention, and reassurance. Your mom or dad may not be able
to change some things, but having a talk can really help.

It's true that talking about uncomfortable feelings can be
difficult. It may be embarrassing. It's also possible to just feel

numb. That's because our minds have a way of protecting us by shutting out feelings when they are too strong. You may think you want to keep your feelings to yourself. But if your feelings are affecting your schoolwork and relationships, then it's time to talk about them.

HOPES AND WORRIES ABOUT PARENTS

Most kids hope their parents will find a way to work things out with each other. But if one parent starts to date, you may feel disappointed. You may have to face the thought that your parents may not get back together again. All of the feelings about your family breaking apart may come up again. You may also feel sorry for the parent who is not dating, or be afraid that the parent who isn't dating will be angry or sad.

Kids want parents to be strong, and may even want to protect them to help them be strong. So when a parent is sad or angry, some kids think they have to make everything better. Or they may want to avoid an upset parent, because it's hard to cope with how it feels when a parent is upset. If one parent is happier than usual, and the other parent seems lonely or sad, a kid can feel uncomfortable around both of them. This is one of those situations that make divorce especially hard for kids.

FEELINGS ABOUT PARENTS' FRIENDS

When you first meet the people your mom and dad are dating, you may not like them, just because they are not your other parent. And if you do like them, you may feel guilty about it or feel sorry for your other parent. Those situations can be confusing. Sometimes it's hard to know if you don't like the person because you feel guilty about it and sorry for your other parent, or because you genuinely don't like him or her.

If you think about it and decide your parent made a bad

choice, it's hard to have to be around him or her. Talk to your parent about how you feel. Otherwise you may end up trying to show your mom or dad how you feel by behaving negatively or having an attitude that gets you into trouble.

SOME SOLUTIONS

Here are some things to think about and do when your parents begin dating new people.

- Telling your parents what you are feeling can be a great relief.
- It's best if you are polite to their new friends and have an open mind about them. New people in your parent's life will never replace the other parent in your life, so you don't have to compare them or worry about liking them.
- When the situation allows, you might feel more comfortable having a friend of your own over when your parent's friend is visiting.
- If you feel guilty about liking a person your parent is dating, you can admit to your other parent that you like the parent's new friend, but you know that he or she will never be the same as being with your real mom and dad.
- Remember that your parents are grown-ups, and they are responsible for handling their own problems and feelings. If one of your parents is dating and the other isn't, it's not your job to protect your non-dating parent or somehow try to make that parent feel better.
- If you need time alone with your mom or dad, ask for it. Ask if you can have dinner or be together a couple of times a week, and not with anyone else. Make sure you get your alone time with each of your parents.
- It's okay to tell your parents that it bothers you when they

have long phone conversations with their friends while you're around. If it's taking away from time you need with them, or if you are hearing conversations you'd rather not listen to, it's important to say so.

• If you're nervous about telling your parent what's on your mind, it might help to talk to another adult first, such as your school counselor, another family member, a family friend, or the parent of one of your close friends.

• Just like Ginny learned, you can't always expect your friends to understand how something feels if they haven't gone through it themselves.

• Sometimes it helps to write in a journal or imagine talking to someone who would understand.

• Ask your parents to find a support group for you so you can talk with other kids who have experienced divorce in their lives. Often your school counselor will form such a group.

• If you need extra help sorting out all your feelings, ask your parents to find a psychologist or other therapist you can meet with and talk to. Therapists are experts at helping you figure out feelings and find healthy ways to deal with them.

In the meantime, be sure to focus on your own friendships and on the positive things in your life that make you happy.

—Mary Lamia, Ph.D., is a clinical psychologist in the San Francisco area and the host of the call-in program KidTalk with Dr. Mary *on Radio Disney-San Francisco/Sacramento.*

About the Author

MARY COLLINS GALLAGHER, L.P.C., is an elementary and middle school counselor who has worked with hundreds of children before, during, and after their parents' divorce. She has three grown children and lives in the Washington, D.C., area.

About the Illustrator

WHITNEY MARTIN's illustrations have appeared in books, magazines, and catalogs, and he has worked on many animation projects, including Walt Disney movies. Before his career as an artist, he was a sergeant in the U.S. Marine Corps Reserves. Whitney now lives in Santa Fe, New Mexico, with his wife and two children.